Alvin Webster's
Surefire Plan for Success

(and How It Failed)

Books by Sheila Greenwald

All the Way to Wit's End
It All Began with Jane Eyre:
    Or, The Secret Life of Franny Dillman
Give Us a Great Big Smile, Rosy Cole
Blissful Joy and the SATs: A Multiple-Choice
    Romance
Will the Real Gertrude Hollings Please Stand Up?
Valentine Rosy
Rosy Cole's Great American Guilt Club
Alvin Webster's Surefire Plan for Success (and How
    It Failed)

Alvin Webster's Surefire Plan for Success

(and How It Failed)

by

Sheila Greenwald

Joy Street Books
Little, Brown and Company
Boston   Toronto

First Edition

Library of Congress Cataloging-in-Publication Data
Greenwald, Sheila.
    Alvin Webster's surefire plan for success (and how it failed)

    "Joy Street books."
    Summary: Gifted fifth grader Alvin Webster, accustomed to always being
the best, the first, and the one with the most right answers, has some ad-
justments to make when he finds out he is getting a new baby brother at
the same time he tries to tutor a less gifted student who does not want to
be tutored.
    [1. Gifted children — Fiction.   2. Competition
(Psychology) — Fiction.   3. Schools — Fiction.
4. Babies — Fiction]   I. Title.
PZ7.G852Am 1987   [Fic]   87-3625
ISBN 0-316-32706-9

BP

Published simultaneously in Canada
by Little, Brown & Company (Canada) Limited

Printed in the United States of America

30466

For my mother,
Florence Greenwald

Chapter One

It was the Monday before Thanksgiving when we sat down to dinner that Dad said, "We have some wonderful news to share with you, Alvin." He handed me a big box. "It's a present." I checked for air holes. Maybe it was the guinea pig I wanted, that they said I couldn't have because of the mess. I would call him Harold. I couldn't wait to open it. I love presents.

At least I used to.

Mom hugged me. "You're going to be a big brother. I know you'll be the best big brother in the whole world."

"How can I be best when I never even studied for it?"

"You don't have to study for it," Mom assured me. "Just stay the giving, caring, loving, sharing person you already are."

"I am?"

"You know how much you love your cousin Molly and care for your classmates at school."

Love Molly? I love to beat her at checkers. Care for my classmates? I care if one of them gets a better grade than I do. What was she talking about?

Dad said, "Mom and I are taking a course in birthing and parenting. These books and posters will help you with brothering. When the time comes, we'll all be ready to welcome the baby."

"The baby" — Mom beamed — "is a boy. We know because a test was done that showed him on a screen. His name is Alexander Herbert Webster."

He wasn't even born yet, and he was in a movie?

MOVIE THEATRE
STARRING
ALEXANDER WEBSTER
IN
THE BABY

For me they had a scrapbook called *Our Baby* and they didn't start it till I was one week old. "Where will you put him?" I asked.

"I've brought your crib and dresser up from the basement storage room. They fit perfectly in my old study. It will be Alexander Herbert's new room."

Already he had a new room, my old furniture, and a name.

"So how does it feel to be called Big Brother?" Dad asked me.

Big Brother? What happened to Alvin? I liked it better. I liked my old crib and dresser. I liked Mom's study. I liked not having to give and share, but I nodded my head. "It feels fine," I lied.

Just for the record, my name is Alvin Webster. I live on the Upper West Side of Manhattan, near the Hudson River, and I take the crosstown bus to my school. That is because I am in the Gifted Child Program at the Foxbrite Model Elementary School for Boys.

I took the test for Foxbrite when I was five. I have no problem with tests or sports or games. My parents say, "Everything Alvin does, he does best. He is a born winner."

I always figured that was why they didn't have to have another kid. I mean, who needs a sticky dribbler like my cousin Nicholas, or a doofus like my cousin Molly, when they've got ME?

Guess what? I figured wrong.

The morning after I found out about Alexander (the movie star) Webster, I saw Danny Trout on the crosstown bus. Danny and I are in the same class at the same school. We get practically the same grades. Since we have so much in common you'd think we'd be friends. But another thing we have in common is: we don't like each other.

"I got ninety-five on the math test," Danny called to me. "What did you get?"

"Ninety-eight," I said. I knew that this meant Trout's nose would start to twitch and he would call me Alvie and begin to swing his foot till he kicked me by accident. Also, he would accuse me of cheating.

"Say, Alvie . . ." Trout swung his foot. "How come you got such a terrific grade and you look so awful? Are you guilty or something? What's on your mind?"

I decided not to talk about what was on my mind. If you don't talk about something, sometimes it goes away.

Sometimes —

but not always.

In school we had our midterm awards assembly. As usual, I won the medal for history, but this year I won the medal for math, too.

Now that they were all wrapped up in Alexander Herbert I wondered if my parents would even care. I wondered if anybody would care. Danny Trout did.

"Hey, wait a minute!" He waved his hand at Dr. Olmstead. "My grade-point math average is one point six percentage points higher than Webster's!"

"That is true, Trout," Dr. Olmstead agreed. "But Webster's classwork is excellent. It was so close, and since you won it last year, we thought Webster should have a turn. Also, Trout, it is important that you learn to share. Speaking of sharing," Dr. Olmstead said with a smile, "it gives me great pleasure to tell you boys about a new program that will allow you to share your talents with others."

Sharing again? Was this an epidemic? What happened to winning and being best?

Dr. Olmstead continued. "Each of you gifted boys will be paired up with a regular Foxbrite fifth grader to help him with a subject in which he is doing poorly."

After assembly we each got a piece of paper with a name on it.

"Roger Dunton," Danny cried, waving his paper like a victory flag. "I have great plans for him."

When he saw the name of my student, he hooted, "Oh no, not him!

"He's the dumbest of the dumb. I'll bet you the math medal you won't be able to teach him a thing."

"By the time I'm finished with him, he'll win a math medal of his own," I said.

"You haven't even met him yet," Danny warned.

"It doesn't matter." I was getting excited. "This is my big chance."

"For what?"

"To prove that I'm best at giving and sharing." Since giving and sharing were suddenly so important to my parents, what could be better?

"When I got back to homeroom, I drafted my three-pronged strategy:

I couldn't think of number three, but I wasn't worried. First I'd work on one and two.

Chapter Two

The next day after lunch, we went to study hall to meet with our students.

"This is Robert Bone. Robert, Alvin won the math medal this year. He'll help you with that troublesome subject," Dr. Olmstead said.

I suddenly had a feeling this might be harder than I thought.

But I tried to be really friendly. "Glad to meet you, Robert," I put out my hand. "Do they call you anything for short?"

"They call me Robertson Wheatly Nelson Bone."

We sat down at a long table in the study hall.

At the end of the table, Danny's Roger was already busy taking notes. I made a page of sample problems and gave them to Bone. He worked on them so hard he was sweating. With this kind of effort, I'd have him winning a math medal in no time. I might as well check off the first item of my Three-Pronged Strategy. One down and two to go.

I should have known better.

"Robertson." I tried to stay calm. "Just why did you draw birds instead of doing the math?"

"Because I'm very good at birds and my math is awful." He grinned.

"Can I see your workbook?" When he handed it to me, I was sorry I had asked. "These answers are all wrong."

"The birds did them."

"The birds are going to need to work a lot harder."

"They work hard at nest building and food gathering and survival. The important things." The bell rang. Bone put his terrible workbook into his knapsack and stood up. "Getting the right answers in a math workbook doesn't interest them."

That night Uncle Todd and Aunt Libby came to dinner with my cousin Nicholas. All Nicholas does is scream and wet and spit up, but everybody just smiles and says, "Oh, you wonderful, adorable baby."

They call him Nick-Nick for short. I think Nit-Wit suits him better. When they leave, everything is sticky and has a bad smell, including me.

"How do you feel about being a big brother?" Aunt Libby asked me.

"Just great," I lied. "I can't wait."

"Then here you go," she said, as she put Nit-Wit on my lap. "You can start to practice right now." Suddenly I remembered that honesty is the best policy.

He kept squirming around. I wished somebody would take a picture of us for the album.

I wished somebody would take him away. Giving and sharing was going to be harder than I'd thought. I had to learn THIS?

When we finally sat down to dinner, Uncle Todd asked me about school. Since he's a college professor like my parents, I told him about my problem with Bone.

"What you have to do is reach him through his interests," Uncle Todd said.

"The birds," Mom agreed. "Try to reach him through his interest in the birds."

"Why don't you keep a journal of your progress with him?" Uncle Todd suggested. "It could be a fascinating document."

"The teaching experience from the point of view of a bright fifth grader." Mom's face seemed to be shining with a special light, the way it did when I scored tops in an aptitude test and got accepted to the gifted class. The way it did when she told me about Alexander Herbert.

"Maybe a university press would want to publish it." Uncle Todd laughed. "I can just see it in the window of the Teacher's College Book Store."

Dad laughed, too. "Who knows, we'll see."

I knew. I could see as if it were right in front of me.

It was the third fantastic thing

I needed for my Three-Pronged Strategy.

Over Thanksgiving vacation my parents gave me some books to read that they thought would help with the Bone project.

The books had some great ideas.

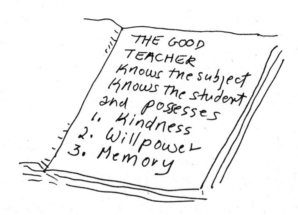

THE GOOD
TEACHER
Knows the subject
Knows the student
and possesses
1. Kindness
2. Willpower
3. Memory

There was no way I could fail. I made an outline and a shopping list. I shopped all Saturday afternoon.

Monday morning I brought the stuff I had bought to school and put it in my locker. Later in the day, before study hall, I took it out and ran with it to the library. I wanted to be all set when Bone walked in. He was fifteen minutes late, but I could tell right away I had his interest.

"What's up?" Bone asked.

"I am a teacher bird and you are my learning bird. I am going to teach you about the wonderful world of math. Every time you answer correctly, you will receive a bird seed. For ten bird seeds you will get a jelly bean," I explained.

"I have a better idea," Bone said. "Let's forget about the wonderful world of math and the bird seed and skip to the jelly beans."

"Okay, then, you can have a jelly bean to start." I was trying to be kind.

"Tweet, tweet," said Bone.

"That's enough," I said. Things were getting out of hand. It was time for willpower.

Trout and Dunton were making funny noises. "I did that stuff with jelly-bean rewards in kindergarten," Dunton hissed in a fake whisper.

"I did it in nursery school." Trout didn't bother to whisper.

Bone's face got very red. Even his eyes looked red. "This isn't nursery school. I'm no learning bird and you're no teacher bird from the wonderful world of math. You're a nerd bird who thinks he's hot stuff because of winning some dumb medal."

I stopped being kind. Willpower was no help. It was time for memory. "For your information, please remember I'm Alvin Webster, top-ranking fifth grader in the Foxbrite Gifted Child Program, and you better pay attention because you're my assigned student. I'm going to give and share my talents with you whether you like it or not!"

"I'd rather you gave and shared your jelly beans," Bone said, and he grabbed the whole bag and stuffed it into his knapsack. I tried to pull it out, but Mrs. Notkin, the librarian, told us we were making too much noise, just as the three o'clock bell rang.

When I got outside, Trout and his sidekick Bender and Dunton were already standing at the corner waiting for the bus. So was Bone, stuffing beans in his mouth.

When he saw me, Bender began to wave

his arms around as if they were wings. "Puck, puck, puck," he cried, doing his chicken imitation.

I pretended not to notice, so he flapped over to Bone. "Say, birdie, can I have a bean?"

"He's not a birdie, and they aren't his beans." I was getting fed up.

Trout crowed, "He's a bean-eating booby bird and you're his trainer . . . I mean, tutor. You picked a loser, Webster."

Bone stopped chewing and handed me back my bag of jelly beans. "Webster didn't pick me. He drew me, like in a raffle."

"That's right," I agreed. "I got Bone the same way you got Dunton."

"Only my Dunton can add and subtract," Trout bragged, "and your Bone can't count to ten."

"My Bone can too count to ten."

"Is that why you gave him jelly beans?" Bender pushed his face up to mine. "Gimme a bean, teacher . . . one, two, three . . ." He started counting. When he got to ten, I gave him some beans.

Giving and sharing was more fun than I thought. Jelly beans were bouncing all over the sidewalk. Bender picked up a bunch and threw them back at me. Soon everybody was throwing them.

Just when I was about to throw another
handful, Mr. Phillips, my homeroom teacher,
came out of school. "What's going on here?"
he said.

"It's all because of Webster tutoring Bone,"
Trout whined, "and pretending to be a bird."

"Perhaps you could find some better method of tutoring, Alvin." Mr. Phillips stared at me.

I backed up until he'd turned to go into the school.

Trout waved. "You lose, Alvie. I told you he was hopeless."

Everybody was gone except for me and Bone. He picked up the spiral notebook that was supposed to be my record book for keeping track of his progress. Some progress. "That was good jelly-bean throwing," he said. He handed me the book. "Why did Trout say, 'You lose'?"

"He bet me my math medal that you were a moron and would never be able to learn math," I confessed.

Bone sat down on the sidewalk next to his knapsack. There were jelly beans stuck to his pants. "I wish I didn't hate it so much when people call me a moron or a bird brain. It makes me do stupid things."

"Like what?" I asked him.

"Like try to prove they're wrong." He opened his scribbled-over workbook. "What do I have to know for that final anyway?"

I showed him the list of the chapters:

Adding Fractions

Subtracting Fractions

Multiplying
and
Dividing Fractions

He studied it.

"We'll work together," I said, getting excited again. "I'll come to your house. You'll come to my house. I have a plan."

Bone picked a jelly bean off his knee. "I'm sorry about taking the jelly beans."

"That's okay," I assured him. "They didn't work the way I thought they would."

But they did work:

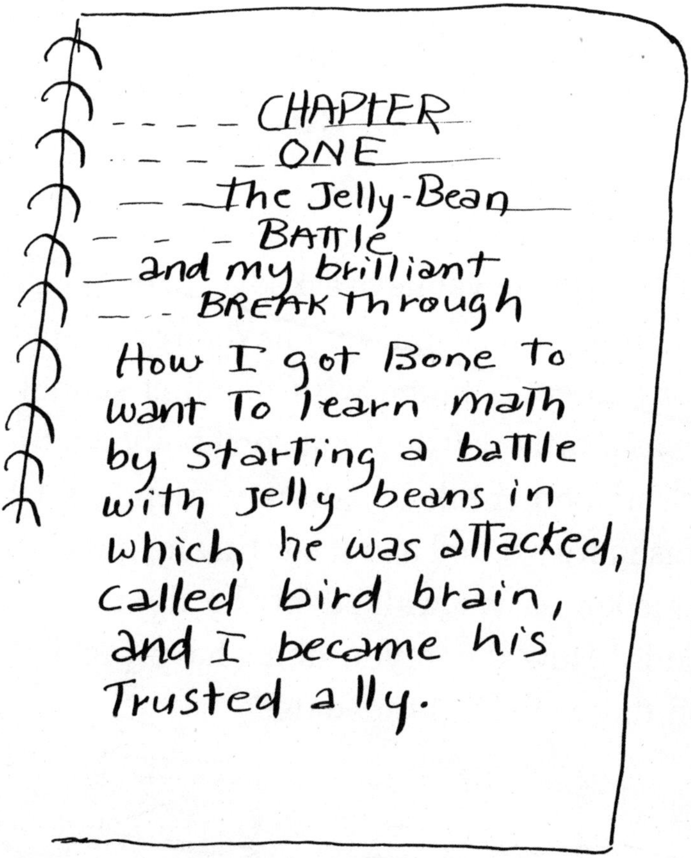

_ _ _ _ _ CHAPTER
_ _ _ _ ONE
_ _ The Jelly-Bean
_ _ _ _ BATTle
_ and my brilliant
_ _ _ BREAK Through

How I got Bone to
want To learn maTh
by starting a battle
with jelly beans in
which he was attacked,
called bird brain,
and I became his
Trusted ally.

41

Chapter
Three

Though I never have asked a Foxbrite regular to my place, the very next day I invited Bone to come home with me after school. I was a little worried that somebody would see us and think he was my friend, but I was more excited about starting my project. As soon as we walked in the door, Bone said, "How come you don't have pictures on the walls, only medals?"

42

In the kitchen he was really upset. "Why are your grades all over the bulletin board?"

"Because they're so good."

"But they aren't beautiful like pictures or even useful like pots and pans. Who wants to look at them?"

"My parents."

In my room he saw my work schedules and plan sheets. "Don't you ever goof off?"

"My day is full of challenging projects so I don't get bored," I explained.

"When I get bored I think about something to draw."

Thinking about something to draw didn't help much with adding fractions.

"How did you get these answers?" I asked him.

"I think I used the B method or maybe the E method where it says to add up the tops and the bottoms, or maybe the bottoms to the tops. Webster, I have a headache. I have to go home."

Before he left, Bone tore a page out of his notebook. It was one of his bird drawings. "This is my favorite." He handed it to me. "It could really help your wall space."

Later, I told my parents how Bone thought we ought to have pictures on the walls. I showed them his drawing. Dad seemed to like it. "It's very good." He sounded surprised.

"I'm sure Alvin could do just as well if he wanted to," Mom said quickly.

After dinner I decided I wanted to.

Mom was wrong, but it didn't matter. After all, drawing pictures didn't count. What counted was teaching Bone how to do fractions and finishing my book and being Alvin Webster "Best" again. Kindness, willpower, and memory were no help. Just when I thought I was making headway, Bone had to start worrying about what was on our walls. It wasn't fair. I had to work and worry while Alexander Herbert only had to keep growing.

45

In the morning, I noticed my parents had tacked something new to the bulletin board.

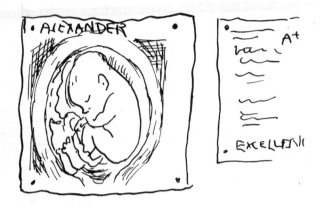

It was a picture, all right. Just in case I forgot to think about the movie star while I ate my breakfast.

But who could eat?

That afternoon, when I went to Bone's place, I could see more problems. No school prizes hung in the hallway. No snapshots of him winning medals, only Bone's bird pictures. No grades on the kitchen bulletin board, no kitchen bulletin board, for that matter. Only birds and pots.

Mrs. Bone came in. "Hi," she said, shaking my hand. Hers was sticky and had a funny smell. "Robertson, who's your friend?"

"He's not my friend, he's my math tutor, Alvin."

"While you're at it, Alvin, could you teach Robertson to keep his jacket clean and his buttons from popping off his shirts and his shirts from popping out of his trousers?" She gave Bone a hug. "Of course math and buttons aren't everything. Robertson is so gifted. Have you seen his birds?"

Gifted? Was she kidding? "Yes, all over his workbook." She laughed as if I had said something funny. She didn't ask if he'd had a quiz that day, or what his grade was, or if she could see it, or check his assignment, or go over his study schedule. She didn't seem to care.

When we went into the living room, I knew why.

"Meet the twins," Bone said.

TWINS? I began to feel dizzy. Could this happen to me?

"I hope you don't mind baby-sitting," said Mrs. Bone, putting on her coat. "I've got to do some shopping. They'll be quiet."

Bone rolled the twins into the kitchen. We sat at the table, which was sticky and had a bad smell. I opened the notebook of special problems I'd made up for him. I started with a simple one which he could easily solve and which would build his confidence. Then I would carefully lead up to the fractions.

"Harry counted sixteen birds' nests. Each nest held three eggs. How many eggs did Harry see?"

"Eggs are good when they're fried" — Bone smacked his lips — "but I'd rather have something else."

"The question is multiply or divide," I reminded him.

"The question is what to eat. I can't work on an empty stomach."

He opened the refrigerator and took out milk and apple juice.

"I came here to do math," I said as calmly as I could.

"But I can't think when I'm starving." He peeled a banana, plugged in the blender, and found a measuring cup. "I'm going to fix us a Banana Apple Smoothie Surprise."

"By the time it's ready, I'll have to go home and we won't have done any work," I said. I was getting desperate.

"Please don't interrupt." He began to pour

milk into the measuring cup. "Because you're here, I'll just double the recipe. Three quarters of a cup of milk plus one quarter of a cup of apple juice will make one cup of the Apple Smoothie part."

"Hey, wait a minute, you're adding fractions!" I said. "I thought you didn't know how."

Bone poured out the milk as if he hadn't heard me. "So to make two cups of Smoothie, it's three quarters twice, or six quarters, which is one and a half cups. And half a cup of apple juice."

"That's MULTIPLYING," I hollered. "We're not even up to that yet. What's going on here?"

"I told you, I'm making a Banana Apple Smoothie Surprise." Bone looked scared.

"For your information, you are adding and multiplying fractions." I crumpled up my stupid problems and threw them in the trash. "That's what I was going to teach you. I worked out a whole lesson plan. I brought all this stuff. I wasted my time."

"I'm sorry," Bone apologized. "I didn't know making Smoothies was math. I can't do math. I never could. I wasn't lying. Believe me."

"I'll prove it." I took the problems out of the trash and redid them as Apple Smoothie recipes. "If I have half a cup of milk and need a full cup, how many quarters to make it full?"

"Two quarters."

"You see, you do too know how."

"I do?" said Bone in amazement. He grabbed the sheet away from me. "Let me try the rest."

When he finished, I checked his answers. They were all correct.

"I always thought I had to know a method for math, only I could never remember which method. I didn't know I could just use my brains." He turned on the blender and gave each of the twins a piece of banana. They threw them into the blender.

That was the surprise.

"They love that part," Bone said. He poured out glasses for us and bottles for them. Before I could stop him, he handed me the one called Laura and took the one called Nora. At first I thought she was just Nit-Wit with a bow,

but that wasn't how it worked out. "She really likes you," Bone said. Funny thing was, I liked her, too.

Bone was lucky. He had good babies. For all I knew, the last of the good babies. You could tell they hadn't been in movies or taken other people's old furniture. They were sweet.

When Mrs. Bone came home, she asked if I could stay for dinner. I almost said yes, but I had to begin:

CHAPTER TWO
I TURN A FAILING MESS iNTO
A SUCCESS
KiNDNESS and willpower pay off.
It happened when I realized:
Bone liked putting Things in
The blender. I cleverly made
up problems That were blender
recipes.
The BANANA APPLE SMOOThie
surprise Teaches fractions,
addition, multiplication all
in one. When I realized
This I knew HISTORY HAD
BEEN MADE...

Chapter Four

At dinner I showed my parents my new chapter.

"This is unbelievable," Mom said.

"You mean exaggerated?"

"Alvin, you're a born teacher. You create an atmosphere of trust and confidence. Instead of humiliating him by telling him he's wrong, you pose simple problems he can solve."

Dad read my chapter. "It sounds as if you had fun with the babies," he said.

"They're good babies." I nodded. "I fed one of them her bottle."

"You fed her a bottle?" Mom was alarmed. "Have you read the chapter 'How to Feed Baby' in *Know Your Sibling*?"

"She's not that kind of baby," I said. "You don't have to read a book to enjoy her."

After supper I rushed through my homework so I could go over my tutorial schedule and write in my teacher's planning log before bedtime.

The next day, Mr. Phillips told me three out of my six math problems were wrong. "What method did you use?" he asked.

"I used my brains," I said.

"Your what?"

"By the way" — I smiled politely — "could I suggest that you not humiliate me by using the word 'wrong'? Why don't you just pose a simpler problem that I can solve and in that way I would find my own mistake?"

He got sort of bug-eyed and turned away without answering me. I wondered if his teaching troubles had something to do with being deaf.

In the lunchroom, Trout and Bender were swapping sandwiches.

"We haven't played the ninth game of the checkers championship yet," Trout grumbled. "You're always busy."

"I suppose I could fit you in this afternoon before my horn lesson. Of course, I'll have to give up a session with Bone, but he can afford it."

When lunch was over, Mr. Phillips made an announcement. "Some of you may be taking your work a little too seriously," he said with a chuckle. "So we've decided to have a party for all you tutors and your students, Friday before exam week. We want to remind you that all work and no play makes John a dull boy, or at least a very high-strung one."

"Who says I'm high-strung?" Trout takes everything personally. "Just because I want the math medal back that I should have won anyway."

"You can forget the math medal," I informed him. "Bone is practically up to algebra."

This news must have really upset Trout. On the bus home, he called me Alvie and kicked me twice and he beat a lady out of the last empty seat. "I got here first, it's mine," he told her.

When the door opened, he knocked a kid down to be the first one out. "Last one to the corner is a putrescent pig." He was nearly killed crossing the street.

At his house, Mrs. Trout greeted us. "Danny, are you feeling all right? Your color is so high. Did Mr. Phillips grade the math?"

"I got one wrong." Danny grimaced.

Mrs. Trout looked at the empty place on the wall where the math medal had hung

the year before. "That's not bad," she said in such a way that Trout's nose began to twitch like a rabbit's, and I thought of my own exam with three right answers out of six.

In the kitchen, Trout opened a box of Oreos and poured out two glasses of milk.

It didn't compare to a Banana Apple Smoothie Surprise. I felt so sorry for him I

let him take the first game. Since Trout's a
sore winner,

I had to beat him twice after that. Then it
was time for my horn lesson.

"You always leave when you're winning," Danny complained. "It's not fair."

"Maybe you're right," I said because he
was so upset.

On the way to my lesson, I realized that
Trout *was* right. It wasn't fair. I could have
been at Bone's place feeding Laura a bottle
and doing math, instead of having to beat
boring Trout at boring checkers.

As soon as I got home, I called Bone. "I have a great idea," I said. "Why don't we keep up the tutoring, even after your test? That way, you'll never fail math again."

Bone groaned. "I don't really mind failing. It isn't so bad."

"What are you talking about? It's the worst."

"It's not the best," Bone conceded, "but it isn't the worst either. It happens. When it does, you could get assigned a tutor who makes you think you have a chance to pass."

"To pass? Is that all? What about being the best? I don't try anything unless I can be best."

"There must be a lot of good stuff you never try."

I couldn't believe it. Bone actually sounded as if he was sorry for me!

"I'm glad you were my assignment," I told him.

"Me too," he agreed.

"So that's settled. I'll see you tomorrow and next Tuesday, Wednesday, and Thursday just for good measure."

"Four times?" Bone sighed wearily. "Okay, if you say so."

"I say so." This gave me an ending for Chapter Three:

Bone couldn't Thank me enough for saving him from a life of failure. He pleaded with me to continue Tutoring him after The finals. He can't wait for our next session and even wanted an extra one. I can't wait for The finals either.
- All work and no play
- Will get Bone ONE
- HUNDRED Percent and
- Make me a
- FAMOUS AUTHOR

Chapter
Five

Even though I tutored Bone three days in a row, the week went by very fast. All of a sudden it was Friday and time for the party.

There was a big punch bowl, lots of Fritos, and pecan chip cookies. There were all the tutors and all the students. There was me, and there was Bone.

I'd had so much success with math maybe I *would* tutor him in shirts and buttons like his mother suggested.

Before I could propose this to Bone, Mr. Phillips said there was time to play one game of Red Rover. I was glad Bone was on my team, even though it made me a little nervous.

Everybody has a different Red Rover technique. Trout turns himself into an arrow. Bender is a catapult. I'm a silver bullet. When Trout yelled, "Let Webster come over," I shot myself across the gym, right between Bender (weak wrists) and Zlotnick (skinny arms), and kept going . . . right to freedom.

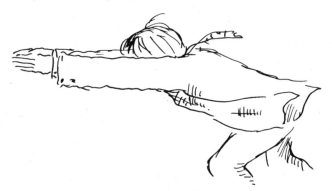

My team cheered and cheered.

Harry Hicks hollered, "Red Rover, Red Rover, let Bender come over."

Bender's catapult ponged right between Monroe and Watkins. They couldn't stop him. Our teams were tied and there was only one minute to go.

Zlotnick bellowed, "Let Bone come over." Bone didn't turn himself into a bullet or an

arrow or a catapult. Bone turned himself
into a bird.

When he got to the other side, he did
something nobody ever did in Red Rover.

Nobody.

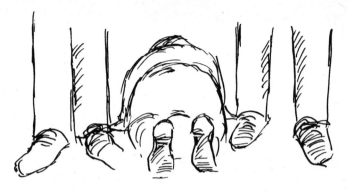

Zlotnick and Luber stopped him.

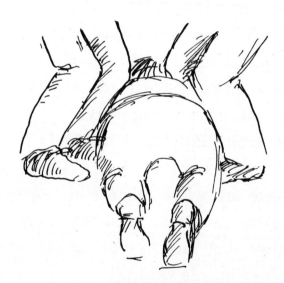

Our team lost.

73

"That was fun," Bone said afterward.

I couldn't believe it. "Fun? We lost the game. We lost because of you."

"But we all had a good time. What difference does it make?"

"It's like the difference between getting an A on the math final and an F."

"Why do you have to get an A? You said it yourself, I know the work."

He wasn't kidding! I suddenly realized that if I wasn't careful, Bone's attitude could sabotage my whole plan. I had better tell him about my book. "You *have* to get an A to prove that The Alvin Webster Surefire Plan for Success works."

"The what?"

"Come over to my place. There's something I want to show you."

Sitting on the crosstown bus with Bone, I began to think. What if he got all emotional and worked up, or broke down with gratitude? What should I say? I was about to make him famous, after all.

Nobody was home. We didn't stop in the kitchen for something to eat. We went right back to my room. I couldn't wait for Bone to see my book.

He sat down at my desk and began to turn the pages. Even though he was reading very slowly,

I could tell

he was moved.

Finally he closed the book and put it down
and left. He didn't say good-bye.

When I called his house later, his mother
told me he wouldn't speak with me.

Chapter
Six

I couldn't figure it out. I wanted the best for Bone. I wanted him to get high marks, just like my parents wanted me to get high marks. All Sunday I went over my book and looked for clues. What could have made him so upset?

I was afraid Bone might do something crazy, like purposely fail the math final. My mother said not to worry. "Everybody wants to be a winner. Everybody wants to be best." Bone wasn't everybody.

Monday morning after my own math final, I went over to where the regular Foxbrite Fives were taking their tests. A few other tutors had the same idea.

"My Dunton is ahead." Trout did his sportscaster imitation. "I can tell, he's-a-grinning. Your Bone looks sick."

"But he just turned a page," Bender pointed out.

"Yeah, he probably filled it with birds."

"He's putting away his pencil," I said, "and he's closing his book."

"And-he's-standing up," Trout howled like it was a home run. "And-he's-a-done."

I wondered what he'd-a-done. He didn't even look at me when he came out the door.

I went home and tried to study, but I couldn't concentrate.

The next day after my English final, Dr. Olmstead called me into his office. Bone was already there.

"Congratulations, Webster, on a splendid job." He shook my hand. "Robertson got one hundred on the exam." He shook Bone's hand. "We all knew how gifted he was, but none of us dreamed anybody could get him to work on a subject he didn't like. It's a miracle."

Why didn't Bone say, "*It's no miracle, it's Alvin Webster's Surefire Plan for Success?*" Instead, he stared at his test paper and the big one hundred that was circled in red, as if it was a magic act.

I was so excited; the first part of my Three-Pronged Strategy had succeeded. I ran down the hall to my class. I couldn't wait to see my own math score. Mr. Phillips was handing out the results of our final. I smiled as he gave me mine. He didn't smile back. Was he having eyesight trouble now?

There had to be a mistake. Then I saw that there were — forty of them, forty out of a hundred, and all of them mine.

I knew right away the second prong of my Three-Pronged Strategy had collapsed. Disaster.

I was Big Brother from now on. I felt sick. I wanted to go home and close the door to my room and never open it again. But when I got home and into my room, I felt even sicker.

The kitchen was worse.

I didn't know what to do with my test paper. Finally, I thought of a good place to hang it.

But what would I tack on the bulletin board?
I found an old test and changed the date on
it. It looked kind of smeared so I spilled a
little juice on top. I thought my parents might
recognize some of the questions so I stepped
on them.

When my mother came home, I showed her my exam. "I dropped it in the street and Trout ran over it," I said.

At dinner, Dad congratulated me, "but the test looks as if it's been to war."

"It fell down in the lunchroom and Bender spilled his lunch on it." I laughed as if this was funny. Then I saw Mom's face and remembered what I had told her.

After dinner, I went to my room to study

for my last final. But I couldn't. When I got into bed, I couldn't sleep. In the middle of the night I was still up.

In the morning, Mom said, "Alvin, is there something bothering you that you would like to talk about?"

How could I talk about failing math and becoming Big Brother instead of Alvin and losing Bone as a friend?

I was glad my last exam was in history. History is my favorite subject. For a little while, I forgot about my problems and tried to remember some of the ones George Washington had. When the test was over, Trout and Bender asked me to go for pizza. I knew they would review all the questions and fight about who had gotten the right answer. I used to like that because I was always right. Now I wasn't so sure. I just wanted to go home.

At the bus stop I saw Bone. He took something out of his knapsack. "I've been meaning to give you this," he said. "It's yours as much as it is mine." The bus came and we both got on.

I looked at his hundred percent paper. It *was* half mine. "We could celebrate your score with a Smoothie," I suggested.

Bone shook his head. "You're not my tutor anymore, and after I read that success book, I found out you've never been my friend."

"What was wrong with my book?"

"You make yourself out to be some kind of hero for teaching me how to pass math. Big deal. I told you failing isn't so terrible if you know how to do it. I really feel sorry for you, Webster. Getting a hundred is easy. Failing takes guts. You'll never know." He stood up to get off at his stop.

"But I do know." I grabbed Bone's sleeve and pulled him back to his seat. "Come to my house and I'll prove it."

"I don't have to go to your house." Bone shook me off. "I told you, you're not my tutor anymore and friends don't use each other to write books."

"Next time we'll write one together," I promised. "That's called a collaboration."

He stayed on the bus.

When I showed Bone my sixty, he wasn't impressed. "You may have failed, but you did it like a coward."

I had to prove to him that I could fail with courage.

After that, we celebrated with a Kiwi Prune Juice Original Smoothie. Bone said it was too bad there weren't any babies to make it a surprise. I told him that soon there would be. I showed him the movie star.

"He's weird." Bone made a face.

"That's because he isn't born yet," I said. "When he's born, he'll be okay."

"Will you tutor him so he passes math?"

"As long as you tutor him in failing it," I said. "Maybe that's more important."

"Here's to Alexander Herbert." Bone raised his glass of Smoothie. "He'll have everything."

That night when we sat down to dinner, Dad said, "We have something to share with you, Alvin." He handed me a big box. "It's a present."

I used to love presents. Now I wasn't so sure.

"Go on, open it," Mom said.

"I thought I couldn't have one because they're messy and nocturnal."

"That could describe babies." Mom laughed. "You were up at night and Alexander Herbert will be too. It doesn't mean we don't love you both."

I looked at Harold and I knew what Mom meant. It didn't matter if he was the worst guinea pig in the world. For me, he was the best.

There were lots of bests. I'd put that in my next book.

And I'd dedicate it to:

LAURA

and

NorA

and

A.H.W.

ALEXANDER HERBERT

with special Thanks
to a new friend